Kittens in the Butter AND THE GRAND Adventure

Malvina Muzichuk

First published in 2022

Written by Malvina Muzichuk

ISBN: 979-8-218-04043-7

booksbymalvina@gmail.com

To my God and Lord Jesus Christ all the glory for
He has given me the creativity.

To my dear parents and twin sister for
always believing in my book.

"This is the day the Lord has made.
Let's rejoice and be glad today!" Psalm 118:24

Monsieur and Madam Meow first fashioned the nickname **kittens in the Butter** for their twin kittens, at one morning's breakfast.

In fact, how Mademoiselle **Daisy** and Mademoiselle **Maisy** came to have such an odd nickname was because they were two of the most **Pampered Kittens** in all of France—and their favorite treat was **butter**.

"Have you heard?" asked Daisy, one Saturday morning, turning to her four-minute older twin.

"About what?" asked Maisy, wiping her mouth with her napkin.

"Aunt E is traveling to London today...by boat," announced Daisy, taking a bite off her croissant.

"Hah!" exclaimed Maisy, "When she isn't traveling, tell me then!"

"Ah, how I would LOVE an adventure," sighed Daisy. "Somewhere faaaaar away."

"Me too," agreed Maisy. "We only travel to new places in our imagination bubbles."

"The Lord has created this day," broke in Madam Meow cheerfully, "so let us enjoy it!"

"That's right," added Monsieur Meow, clearing his throat. "Even if we don't travel far."

But Daisy and Maisy heard nothing.
For they were busily traipsing away on a
new adventure in their imaginations.

"Hello, hello kittens!" called Madam Meow.

"To earth, Kittens in the Butter, to earth," called Monsieur Meow, waving his hand in front of them.

Landing back on earth, Daisy resumed, "You know. Aunt Eloise was just at the sea last week."

"The sea is like a treasure chest with sparkling jewels," said Maisy, imitating her aunt's voice and words.

"Hah! You sound just like her," laughed Daisy.

"I do like anything that sparkles!" announced Maisy.

"One day we'll see another horizon," declared Daisy. "I'm sure of that."

"Soon," added Maisy. "Soon..."

Later, that morning, Daisy and Maisy were slowly tidying up their room.

When suddenly a grand idea danced into their heads.

"Maisy, let's just you and I go to Catonsville Townsquare."

"You know. That's just what I was thinking, Daisy!"

So, with no time wasted, they tiptoed out of their room and quietly shut the door of MEOW Manor.

"Look Maisy!" exclaimed Đaisy, upon their arrival. "Our friends Wisey the Owl and Squirly the Squirrel are here."

They chatted a bit with their friends and hurried away to sightsee the new displays.

"Look Đaisy! Adela's Boutique has new dresses from Paris! Blue, your favorite color; green, cream and pink, my favorite color. And purple, red and..."

But there was no answer. Đaisy was nowhere in sight. "Đaisy?" she called, looking around frantically. "Where are you?"

"Psst. Over here," replied a familiar voice out of a carriage.

"Daisy, what are you doing in there?" gasped Maisy. "Get out. Before the carriage driver returns."

"It's an empty carriage, Maisy. I heard the driver say no one will be in it. He is taking it to another city," she declared, peeking out. "Get in quickly and let's go for an adventure."

"But where is it headed, Daisy?"

"I don't know. But it's going somewhere," said Daisy.

At first, Maisy hesitated but then agreed, "An adventure we want, an adventure we'll have."

Glancing back one more time at the new arrivals, she hurried aboard and they set off.

And soon, they fell fast asleep to the sound of the horses' hooves CLiP–CLOP, CLiP–CLOP.

Dreaming sweetly of the faraway places, they so much wished to see. It was two hours later when they awoke to the cry of seagulls.

"It's the sea!" shouted Maisy, rubbing her eyes, as she peered out of the carriage's window. "Wow, it sparkles magnificently and..."

"Ah! Just like Aunt Eloise said," interrupted Daisy, stretching her arms up in the air. "But we better go before we are discovered."

Carefully opening the carriage's door, they sneaked behind a wooden crate.

"Phew, it smells terrible. SO FiSHY!" complained Maisy, taking her hankie out to cover her nose.

"Sis, its Merville. It's a town of seafood, crabs and fish," consoled Daisy. "It's not going to smell like coffee and pastries."

Everything about the new horizon wonderstruck them. The sea, the sailors, the ships full of cargo, the animal travelers and even the three poodles playing on big crates.

"Oh pinch me, Maisy. Am I dreaming?"

"No, Daisy, you are not. We are here at last!" exclaimed Maisy. "The fishy air pinched my nose to remind me that I am not dreaming."

"Hello Kitts," shouted the three poodles. "You must be new around here."

"We are not Kitts but kittens," protested Maisy, throwing her hands on her hips. "No such name exists."

"Yes, this is our first time," interrupted Daisy. "This is my twin, Maisy, and I am Daisy."

"Welcome to Merville!" said the blue shorts poodle. "I'm Bleu."

"I'm Gre," said the green shorts one.
"I'm Yel," said the yellow shorts one.

"We'll show you around," said Gre.

"When first time in Merville, you must-see Merville's **humongous** cannery," barked Yel.

"We have never seen one before," said the twins.

"**FOLLOW US!** We'll show you," said Gre.

"Daisy, maybe we shouldn't follow," begged Maisy.

"Come on, Maisy. I want to see the inside of a cannery," said Daisy. "And this cannery makes my favorite can of salmon."

"But I don't want to see," cried Maisy.
But Daisy was already inside.

"Welcome to Merville's Cannery, the finest in all of France!" howled the poodles. "**And let the fun begin!**"

Bleu grabbed fish out of the water buckets and **flung** them across the room. Gre **twirled** seafood cans across the floor. And Yel picked up a sack of flour and **hurled** it onto the floor.

"Oh, please stop," begged Maisy. "This is awful! Stop!"

"What a mess," cried Daisy. "**Stop, stop!**"

But the poodles didn't stop. They laughed and battered the surprised twins with flour and water. Sopping wet, Daisy and Maisy tried wringing the hems of their dresses and licking furiously the flour off their furs.

"My dress!" wailed Maisy. "My favorite dress!"

""How are we supposed to go home looking like this?" wailed Daisy.

The poodles' fun came to a sudden end. When the cannery owner Monsieur Jean and the cannery workers returned from lunch. "Who did this?" He hollered. "My cannery is a disaster!"

"They did it," cried the twins, pointing at the culprits.

"I told you, Daisy. We shouldn't follow," cried Maisy. "But no, you really wanted to see."

"Don't remind me, Maisy," cried Daisy.

"You, naughty, naughty dogs," shouted Monsieur Jean, grabbing the poodles by their collars. "You will pay for all the damage. And clean this whole cannery until not one speck of fish scale is seen."

$\mathcal{N}$ow it so happened that Monsieur Charles, a wagon driver for Monsieur Meow, was delivering goods to Merville, that very same morning. But who should he meet but the Meow kittens themselves.

"Maisy and Daisy, how did you ever get here?" asked Monsieur Charles.

"We stowed away on an empty carriage."

"Your parents must be very worried about you," said Monsieur Charles.

"Come along, I'll take you home. And along the way, you can tell me all about your grand adventure.

Arriving back in Catonsville, the weary adventurers were wrapped up in **welcoming hugs** and carried **happily home.**

"You see," began Daisy, settling into her favorite spot on the sofa. "This grand idea danced into our heads to go to Catonsville Townsquare—by ourselves."

"And Daisy was the one in the empty carriage first and then called me aboard," chimed in Maisy, as she dried her milk-stained whiskers. "At first, I was nervous but then I wanted an adventure too."

Every detail of the grand adventure was retold including the disaster in the cannery. Monsieur Meow and Madam Meow just chuckled to themselves and shook their heads in disbelief.

And I don't ever want to be covered in flour and water again." exclaimed Maisy.

"Me too!" agreed Daisy.

"Kittens in the Butter." said Monsieur Meow, smiling widely.

"Indeed," said Madam Meow, smiling back, "Kittens in the Butter."

"Kittens in Flour and Water?" said Monsieur Meow with a teasing twinkle in his eyes.

"Perfect new nickname," laughed Madam Meow, "Kittens in Flour and Water, indeed!"

"Oh, no!" cried the twins with one voice. "No indeed!"

"I rather be called Kittens in the Butter." exclaimed Maisy.

"For it does fit us more," declared Daisy.

About the Author

Malvina Muzichuk based Kittens in the Butter series on her twin sister Mary and herself. The twins were given the nickname Kittens in the Butter by their dear parents. This gave birth to the beloved story of all time.

Kittens in the Butter and the Grand Adventure is the first release of the series. When the twins aren't busy taking an adventure, they enjoy reading and acting on their Youtube Channel StoryTime with Mary and Molly. They reside in North Carolina.

CPSIA information can be obtained
at www.ICGtesting.com
Printed in the USA
LVHW072320050922
727649LV00009B/110